Adam and Eve

and the

Garden
of Eden

I have dedicated this book to the children
of Shapla Primary School.

The Eden Project brings plants and people together.
It is dedicated to developing a greater understanding
of our shared global garden; encouraging us to
respect plants and to protect them.

ADAM AND EVE AND THE GARDEN OF EDEN
AN EDEN PROJECT BOOK 978 1 903 91907 1 (from January 2007)
1 903 91907 X

First published in Great Britain in 2004 by Eden Project Books,
an imprint of Transworld Publishers

This edition published 2006

1 3 5 7 9 10 8 6 4 2

Copyright © Jane Ray, 2004

Eden Project Books are published by Transworld Publishers,
61–63 Uxbridge Road, London W5 5SA,
a division of The Random House Group Ltd,
in Australia by Random House Australia (Pty) Ltd,
20 Alfred Street, Milsons Point, Sydney, NSW 2061, Australia,
in New Zealand by Random House New Zealand Ltd,
18 Poland Road, Glenfield, Auckland 10, New Zealand,
and in South Africa by Random House (Pty) Ltd,
Isle of Houghton, Corner Boundary Road & Carse O'Gowrie,
Houghton 2198, South Africa

THE RANDOM HOUSE GROUP Limited Reg. No. 954009
www.kidsatrandomhouse.co.uk
www.edenproject.com

A CIP catalogue record for this book is available from the British Library.

Printed and bound in Singapore

Adam and Eve
and the
Garden
of Eden

Jane Ray

EDEN PROJECT BOOKS

At the very beginning of the world the earth was a dry and dusty place, where nothing could live and nothing could grow.

So God made a mist which watered the ground all over.

Then, with his great hands, he formed the first man out of the clay of the newly watered earth.

He breathed the breath of life into the man's nostrils, so that he became a warm, living soul. God gave him a name, Adam, which means "earth".

In a place called Eden, God planted a garden for Adam. It was full of plants that were beautiful to look at and good to eat.

In the middle of the
garden stood a fountain.
Two great trees grew nearby,
the Tree of Knowledge and
the Tree of Life.

God warned Adam, "You may eat anything you like except the fruits from the Tree of Knowledge and the Tree of Life. If you eat them, you will die."

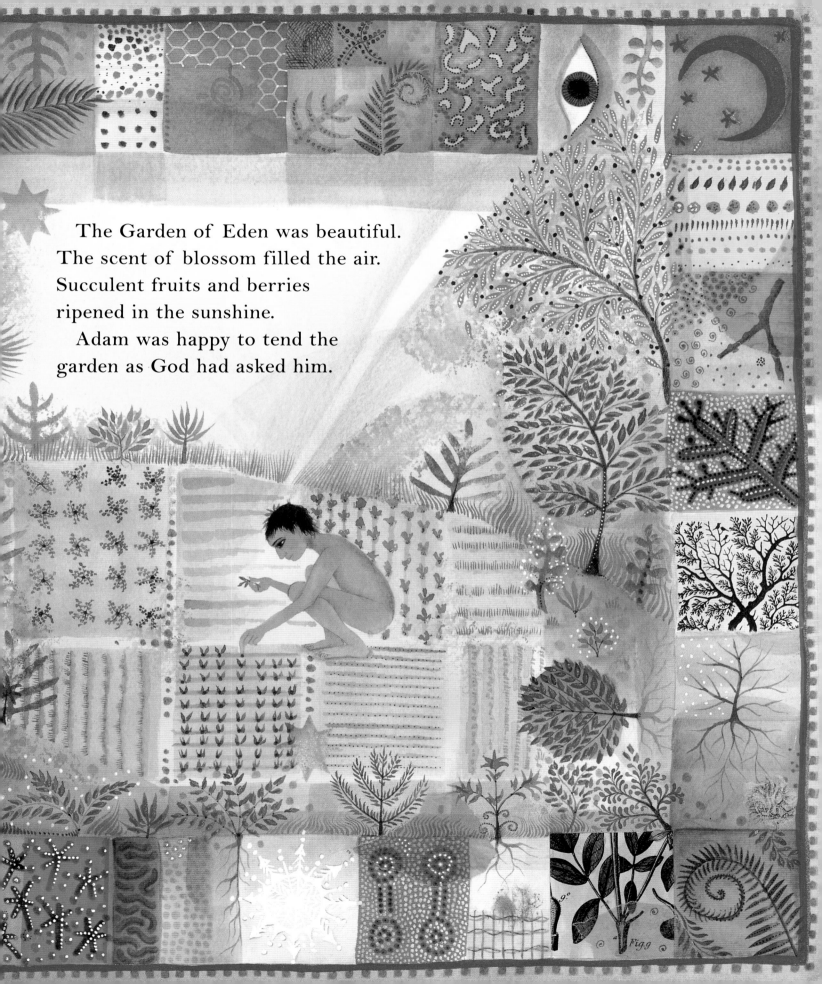

The Garden of Eden was beautiful.
The scent of blossom filled the air.
Succulent fruits and berries
ripened in the sunshine.

Adam was happy to tend the
garden as God had asked him.

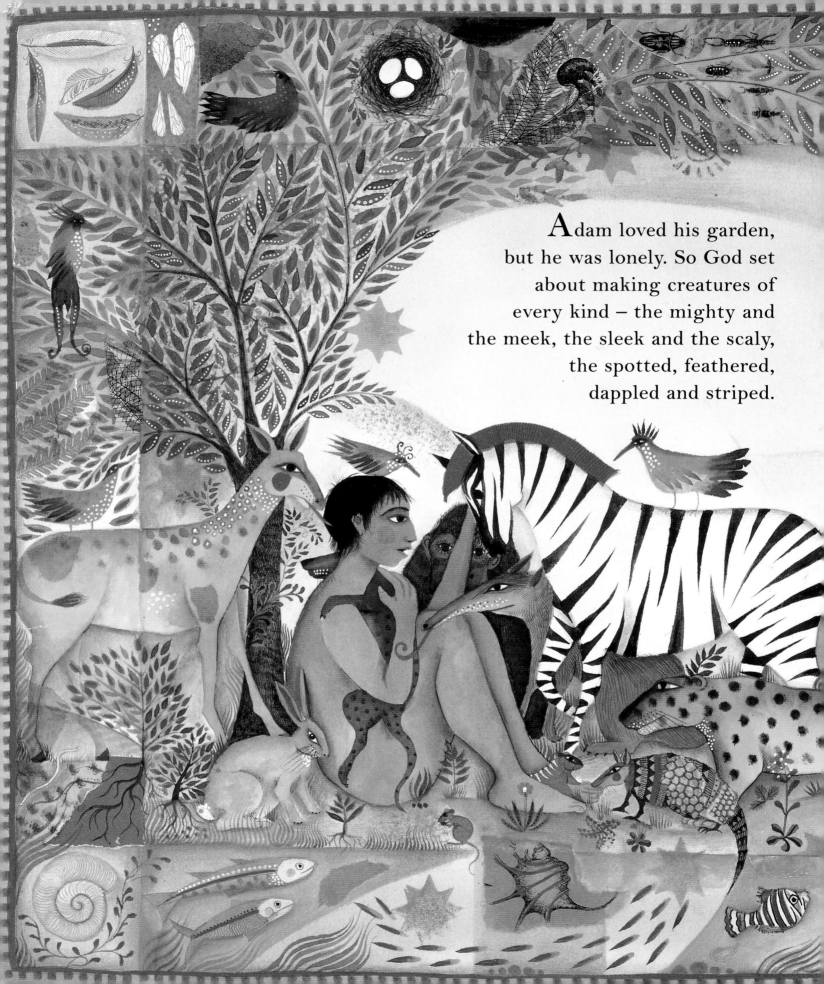

Adam loved his garden, but he was lonely. So God set about making creatures of every kind – the mighty and the meek, the sleek and the scaly, the spotted, feathered, dappled and striped.

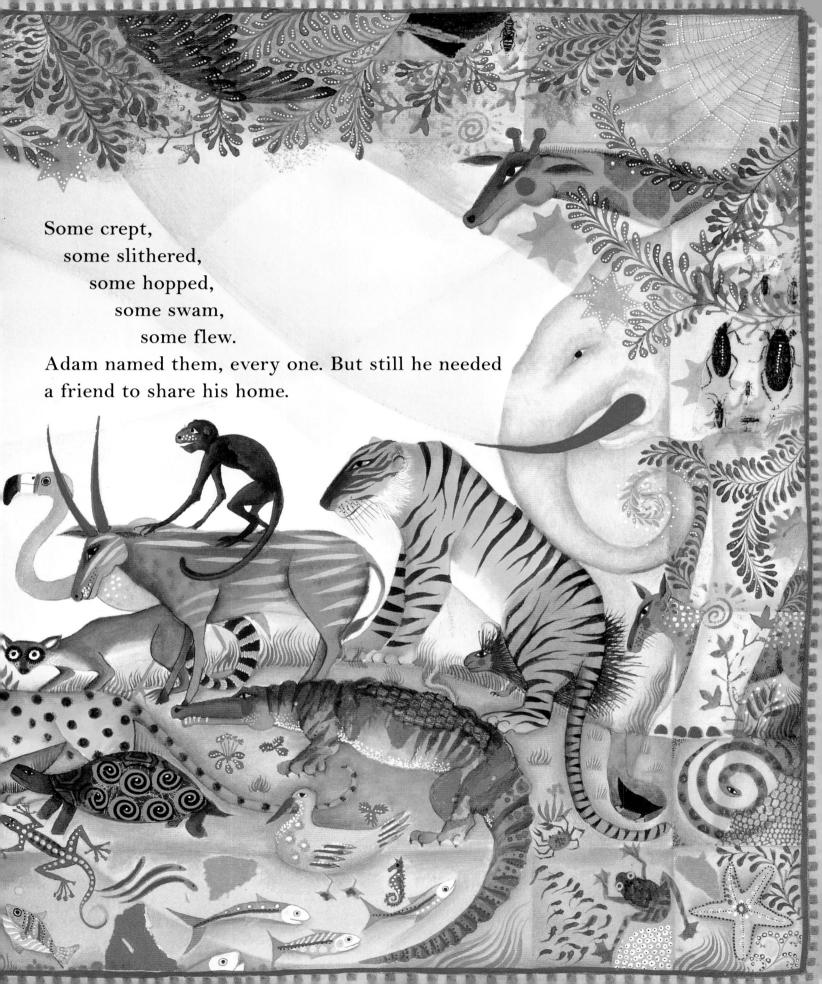

Some crept,
  some slithered,
    some hopped,
      some swam,
        some flew.
Adam named them, every one. But still he needed
a friend to share his home.

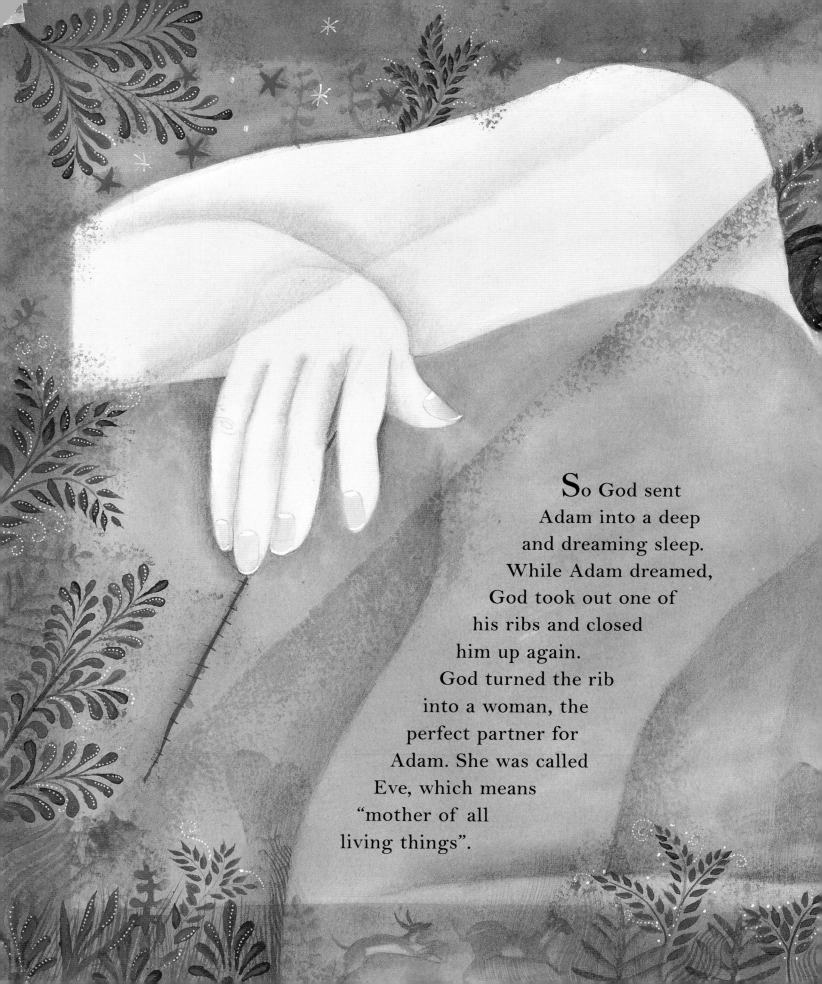

So God sent
Adam into a deep
and dreaming sleep.
While Adam dreamed,
God took out one of
his ribs and closed
him up again.
God turned the rib
into a woman, the
perfect partner for
Adam. She was called
Eve, which means
"mother of all
living things".

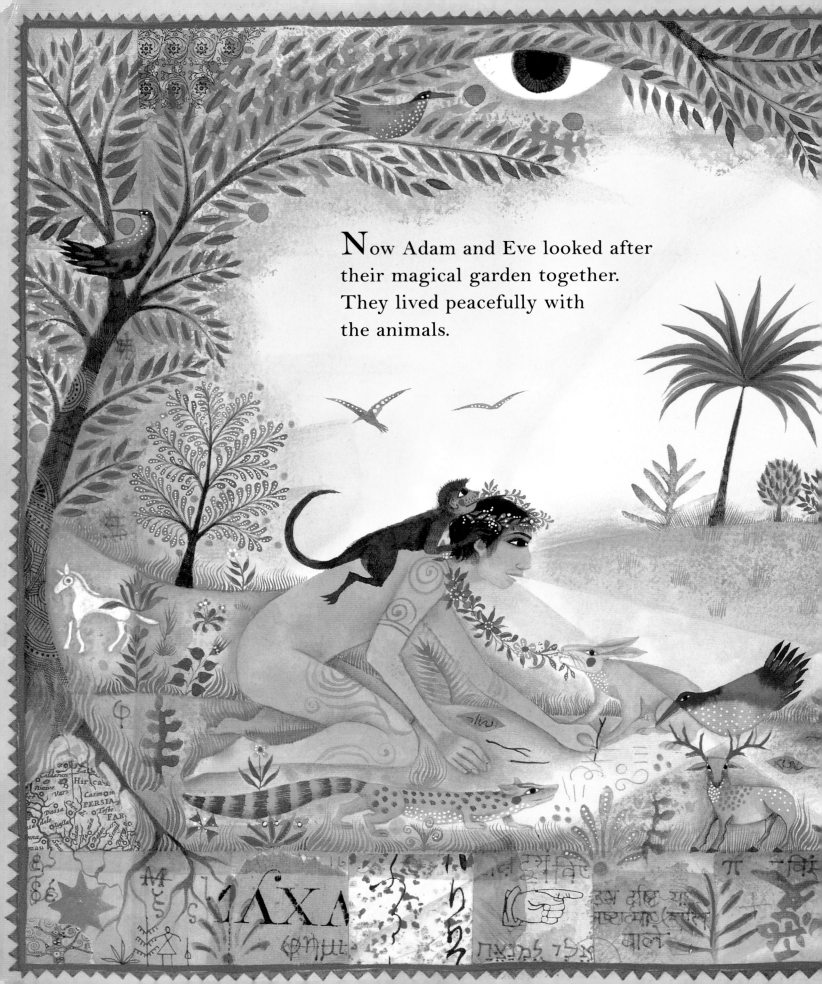

Now Adam and Eve looked after their magical garden together. They lived peacefully with the animals.

They sang and they danced and they
played – and sometimes they simply stood
quietly and gazed at the beauty of it all.
They never, ever, tasted the fruit
from the forbidden trees.

Then, one bright day, as Eve sat alone in
the shade of the Tree of Knowledge,
the serpent appeared beside her.

"I expect God's told you not to eat the
fruit of this tree, hasn't he?" the serpent said.

Eve replied, "We can eat everything else,
but if we eat the fruit from this
tree, God says we'll die."

"Die? You won't die!"
The serpent crept closer
to Eve and whispered,
"The fruit from these
two trees will open
your eyes and make
you wise – like a god.
Wouldn't you like that?"

The serpent melted away into the shadows
and Eve was alone again. Eve looked at
the fruit of the Tree of Knowledge.
Would it really make her wise?

It smelled sweet.
Eve reached out her hand. The fruit was
perfectly ripe.
Eve picked the fruit and bit into its juicy flesh.
When Adam came back, hot and thirsty, they
ate the forbidden fruit together.

As soon as Adam and Eve had eaten the fruit they looked at each other, and for the first time they felt shy.

They quickly found fig leaves and covered themselves up.

Then they heard a voice calling them. It was God, walking in the cool of the garden. Adam and Eve felt ashamed and hid from him in the bushes.

When God saw Adam and Eve
hiding, he guessed that they
had done something wrong.
He told them to come out
from their hiding place.

God asked Adam, "Did you eat
the forbidden fruit?"
"I did," said Adam. "But it was
Eve who made me do it."
"Did you, Eve?" asked God.
"I did," said Eve. "But only because the
serpent persuaded me to."

God was very angry.

"Because of what you have done," he said to
the serpent, "I am going to make you the most
miserable creature on earth. You will slither
everywhere on your belly, and you will
eat nothing but dust."

God turned to Adam and Eve.
"Now you will learn what it is to be sad as well as
happy," he said. "You will work your fingers to the
bone growing food to eat and raising your children.
And when you die, you will return to the earth
from which you were made."

God loved Adam
and Eve as if they were his children,
but he knew that he must send them away
from the Garden of Eden.

"Leave, before you are tempted to eat
the fruit from the Tree of Life," he said.
"You are mortal now, and cannot live
for ever."

God gave Adam and Eve warm
clothes to wear. He handed them some
seeds and cuttings from the garden.
Then he sent them out into the world.

God commanded his angels
to guard the gates of Eden. By the
Tree of Life he set a bright flame, turning
this way and that, like a sword, to protect it.

In the bare earth beyond Eden, Adam and Eve planted a new garden for their family.

*O*ther Eden Project books for you to enjoy:

Global Garden
by Kate Petty and Jennie Maizels

George Saves the World by Lunchtime
by Jo Readman and Ley Honor Roberts

The World Came To My Place Today
by Jo Readman and Ley Honor Roberts

A Child's Guide to Wild Flowers
by Charlotte Voake

My Flower, Your Flower
by Melanie Walsh